A MRS. PIGGLE-WIGGLE ADVENTURE

The Won't-Pick-Up-Toys Cure

ADAPTED FROM THE
MRS. PIGGLE-WIGGLE BOOKS
BY BETTY MacDONALD

ILLUSTRATED BY
BRUCE WHATLEY

HARPERCOLLINS*PUBLISHERS*

The Won't-Pick-Up-Toys Cure
Text adapted from *Mrs. Piggle-Wiggle,*
copyright 1947 by Betty MacDonald,
copyright renewed 1975 by Donald C. MacDonald
Illustrations copyright © 1997 by Bruce Whatley
Printed in the United States of America. All rights reserved.
http://www.harperchildrens.com

Library of Congress Cataloging-in-Publication Data
MacDonald, Betty Bard.
  The won't-pick-up-toys cure / adapted from the Mrs. Piggle-Wiggle books by Betty MacDonald ;
illustrated by Bruce Whatley.
    p.   cm. — (A Mrs. Piggle-Wiggle adventure)
  Summary: Mrs. Piggle-Wiggle suggests a cure for Hubert's bad habit of not picking up his toys.
  ISBN 0-06-027628-2
  [1. Orderliness—Fiction.   2. Cleanliness—Fiction.   3. Behavior—Fiction.]
I. Whatley, Bruce, ill.   II. Title.   III. Series: MacDonald, Betty Bard.
Mrs. Piggle-Wiggle adventure.
PZ7.M1464Wp   1997   96-43610
[E]—dc20   CIP
                                                                                AC

Typography by Al Cetta
1 2 3 4 5 6 7 8 9 10
❖
First Edition

For Kate and Alix

—B.W.

Mrs. Piggle-Wiggle lives here in our town. She has brown sparkly eyes and long brown hair, which she usually wears in a knot on top of her head. She has a dog called Wag and a cat called Lightfoot. But the most remarkable thing about Mrs. Piggle-Wiggle is her house, which is upside down.

All the children love Mrs. Piggle-Wiggle, and Mrs. Piggle-Wiggle loves them. In fact, Mrs. Piggle-Wiggle just naturally understands children, which is of course why all the parents call Mrs. Piggle-Wiggle whenever their children are being difficult. Mrs. Piggle-Wiggle always knows exactly what to do to help cure children's bad habits, like not picking up toys, which was Hubert Prentiss's bad habit.

Hubert was a very lucky boy whose grandfather always sent him wonderful toys for his birthday. Hubert had an electric train with a track that went four times around his bedroom. He had a great big wagon full of blocks, and he had one thousand five hundred toy soldiers. He had a wooden circus, a fire engine with real sirens and lights, and so many books that he had to have two bookcases in his room.

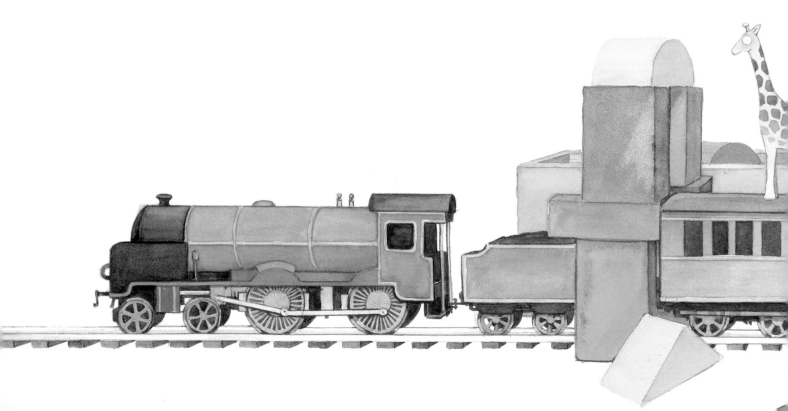

ubert liked all his toys, and he generally shared them with his friends, but he never put them away. When Hubert's mother would tell Hubert to pick up his toys, all he ever did was stuff them under the bed or into the closet. Mrs. Prentiss was getting tired of picking up all of Hubert's toys by herself.

One rainy day Hubert invited his friends over to play. They took out every one of Hubert's toys and played with them all afternoon. Then they went home for dinner and didn't put a single toy away. The next time Mrs. Prentiss opened the door to Hubert's room, she just looked and looked. Then she went downstairs and called Mrs. Piggle-Wiggle.

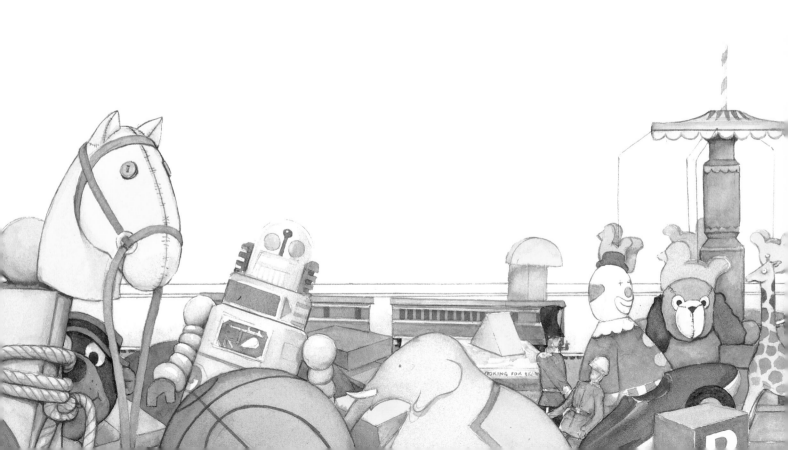

When Mrs. Prentiss told Mrs. Piggle-Wiggle about Hubert's toys, Mrs. Piggle-Wiggle said, "I think that the best thing for you to use is my old-fashioned Won't-Pick-Up-Toys Cure. Starting right now, don't pick up any of Hubert's toys. When his room becomes so messy he can't get out of it, call me."

So Mrs. Prentiss didn't pick up any of Hubert's toys. She baked a chocolate cake instead, and she did not say a word to Hubert about his toys when Hubert's friends came over to play.

The next morning when Hubert came down for breakfast, there was a little pan of paint from his watercolor paint set stuck in his hair. Hubert's mother did not say anything.

The next morning Hubert looked as though he hadn't slept very well. The morning after that Hubert had two pans from his paint set stuck to his hair, and he had a red mark on his cheek that was the shape of one of his blocks. Hubert's mother thought he must have slept on it.

On the seventh day Hubert didn't come out of his room at all. At eleven o'clock his mother got worried and called Mrs. Piggle-Wiggle.

"Hubert must be trapped in his room!" said Mrs. Piggle-Wiggle. "Wait until he calls for food, and then put a piece of dry bread with peanut butter on the garden rake and poke it through his window. He'll have to drink out of the hose."

When Mrs. Prentiss hung up the telephone, she heard Hubert shouting, "Mother, I'm hungry!"

She got a crusty piece of bread, spread some peanut butter on it, and took it around to the side of the house. Soon a hand and arm appeared at Hubert's window. The hand found the bread, grabbed it off the rake, and then banged the window shut. That night Hubert's mother stuck his meat and potato and vegetable on the rake, and his father pushed the hose through the window. It took Hubert a long time to reach the window.

The next day around two o'clock Hubert heard music and children's voices laughing and calling from outside. When he finally managed to look out the window, he saw Mrs. Piggle-Wiggle and all his friends, and right behind them came a circus parade.

"Hurry, hurry, Hubert!" called Mrs. Piggle-Wiggle. "We are all marching to the circus!"

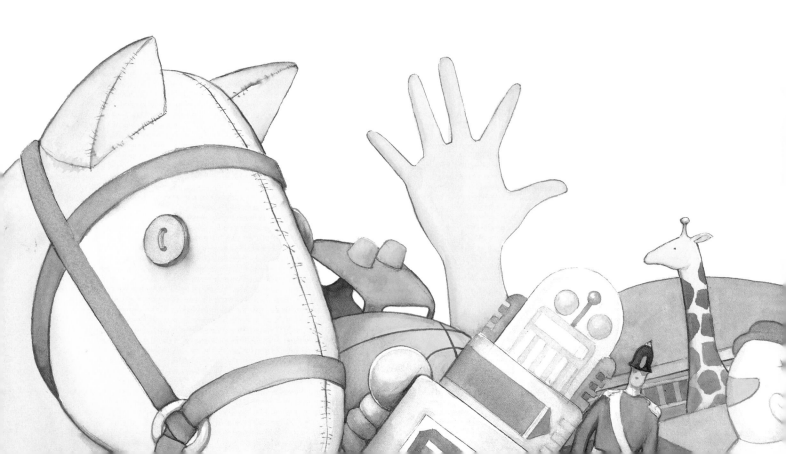

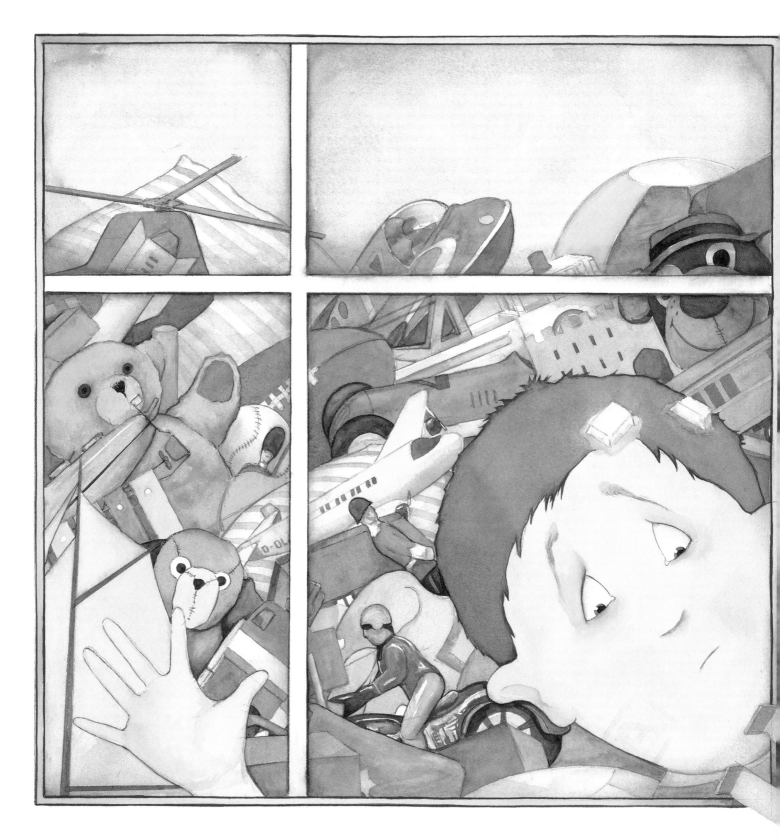

But Hubert couldn't get out of his room! There were too many train cars and blocks and toy soldiers and books in the way. He could hear the music getting farther and farther away, and he began to cry. Then he heard a tap at his window. It was the rake with a note on it.

Dear Hubert,
The only way to get out of that trap is to put everything away where it belongs. If you hurry we will wait for you.
Your friend,
Mrs. Piggle-Wiggle

Hubert put away his blocks, his train cars, his paints, his circus, and his books. He made his bed and put away his toy soldiers. He was just putting away his very last toy when he heard the music again. He put the toy in the box, put the box in the closet, and tore down the stairs and out the front door.

There they came, Mrs. Piggle-Wiggle, all the children, and the circus! Hubert ran out to meet them, and away they went down the street, with Hubert carrying the flag and yelling the loudest. And no one said anything at all about the pan of orange paint stuck in his hair.